Daddy Doesn't Live Here Anymore

A Book About Divorce

By Betty Boegehold

Illustrated by Deborah Borgo

*Prepared with the cooperation of Bernice Berk, Ph.D.,
of the Bank Street College of Education*

A GOLDEN BOOK · NEW YORK
Western Publishing Company, Inc.   Racine, Wisconsin 53404

Note to Parents

Living through a divorce can be shattering for a child. This is partly because of the way children perceive marriage and the family. Adults see their marriage as a relationship between two people, but a child sees his parents' marriage as the thing that gives structure to his entire world. As far as the child is concerned, the end of the marriage could very well mean the end of the world.

A child often thinks that if his parents can stop loving each other, they can also stop loving him. Your child needs much reassurance that this is not so, and that the love parents have for their children is different from the love they have for each other. It is special and it never goes away.

Here are some important things to remember if your family is going through a divorce.

- You don't have to give a child specific reasons for your divorce. A simple explanation is best.
- Don't use your child as a weapon in arguments with your former spouse. It's unfair to the child.
- Keep telling your child how much both of you still love him. Give your child as much reassurance and support as possible.
- Assure your child that the divorce was your decision and your spouse's, and that he or she is in no way to blame for it.
- Your child may feel very angry about the divorce. This is a normal reaction to any great loss. Try and teach your child that anger is not the opposite of love and that one can be very angry at a person one loves very much. That way, the child can deal with his own anger more constructively.
- Your child's behavior may change for the worse, but this, too, is a normal reaction to being frightened and upset. Help your child find constructive outlets for his anger, and try to help him understand that he'll always be loved and cared for.

It is important that both parents continue to give their children love and understanding during this difficult period of adjustment. By reading DADDY DOESN'T LIVE HERE ANYMORE with your child, you can begin to help him define his fears, and then deal with them in a healthy and constructive way.

—The Editors

Casey slowly walked home kicking a little stone along the sidewalk. "I wonder if Mom and Dad are still fighting," she thought. "No. They'll pretend everything is okay. As if I didn't know better!"

Dad's car was gone from the garage. Casey sighed. "At least no one is fighting now."

Inside the house, Casey's mother was vacuuming furiously. Her eyes were red and watery. Mom had been crying again.

"Tough beans!" Casey thought. "If Mom didn't fight so much with Dad, she wouldn't have to cry."

Casey banged her school books down on the hall table
and went to her room. She wandered around, not wanting
to draw, or look at a book, or play with Elmer Elephant.

She stood in front of her old dollhouse. The doll family leaned stiffly against the staircase.

She hadn't played with them in a long, long time. Slowly Casey picked up the mother and father dolls. Then she shook them hard.

"What's the matter with you?" she yelled at them. "Don't you know that parents are supposed to act nice?"

She dropped them back into the dollhouse and picked up the girl and boy dolls. Casey smoothed their hair and straightened out their clothes.

"I'll take care of you," she whispered. "Don't be scared."

"Come to supper, Casey," her mother called. "Soup's on."

Casey's father didn't come home to supper. He didn't come home after supper, either. Casey's mother said softly, "Honey, Daddy's not going to come home. He's not going to live here anymore, because he and I can't get along. We're getting a divorce."

"Daddy doesn't live here anymore?" Casey shouted. "That's mean! Doesn't he love me?"

"He loves you a lot, Casey," her mother said. "He and I just don't love each other anymore. But we both still love you, Casey. You are part of us."

"Tough beans!" Casey yelled. "I liked it the way we were. I don't want to have no daddy." She began to cry.

Casey's mother put her arms around Casey. "Hush, honey," she said. "Daddy will always be your daddy. He'll just live in a different place. You'll see him lots of times, but most of the time, you'll live with me."

Casey pulled away from her mother and ran to her room. She threw the mother and father dolls down on their faces. But she took the doll children to bed with her and Elmer Elephant.

When her mother came in to kiss her good night, Casey pulled the covers over her head and wouldn't kiss back.

Under the covers, she thought, "Maybe I made Daddy go away, so I'll have to get him back. I'll think of something."

By morning, Casey had thought of something. "If I'm sick, Daddy will have to come back. If he loves me."

She grabbed the paint box and painted red spots all over her face. She jumped back in bed and called, "Mommy, Mommy, I'm sick. Get Daddy right away."

Mommy smiled, hugged her, and phoned Daddy.

Daddy was there by ten o'clock. "Please stay here,"
Casey whispered.

"Oh, Casey, darling." Her father held her on his lap and
began to wash off the paint spots. "Mommy and I just can't
live together anymore. You'll come visit me weekends,
vacations—lots of times. You'll feel better later. Wait and
see."

But Casey didn't feel better later. Her stomach hurt because she missed her daddy so much. Even her house didn't seem right anymore.

"I guess Mommy and Daddy don't love me," Casey
thought sadly, "or they wouldn't make me feel so bad.
Maybe I'll run away. Then they'll be sorry they were so
mean. Then we'll have to be a family again."

Casey took Elmer Elephant, some coloring paper, her
crayons, three chocolate-chip cookies, and she ran away.

She ran away across the back yard to the big forsythia
bush. It was so old, its branches hung down to the
ground. Casey crawled under them and hid.

After a while, Elmer Elephant told her he was tired. The
cookies were gone, the papers were all colored, and Casey
was tired, too.

Then Casey's mother pushed aside the branches and sat
down beside Elmer. "Anyone hungry here?" she asked.
"I've got spaghetti and meatballs in the kitchen."
"Will Daddy eat with us too?" Casey asked.

Casey's mother sighed. She said, "Casey dear, you know
he won't. But you'll see him this weekend."

Casey looked at the ground. "Did I do something bad?"
she asked. "Did I make Daddy go away?"

Casey's mother put her arms around Casey. "Never!"
she said. "You are a wonderful girl, Casey, and you
didn't do anything at all to make us get a divorce.
Remember how we used to fight so much, and how you
hated it? I guess Daddy and I just stopped loving each
other."

Casey whispered, "Maybe you'll stop loving me, too."

"Not in a million, zillion years," her mother said. "Your daddy and I will always love you, Casey. The way we love you is a different love, a part-of-us love."

Casey stood up. It was all too hard to understand. "I'm hungry," she said. "Let's eat."

That night in her room, Casey put the mother doll in
one bedroom and the children in their rooms. "Good
night, sleep tight," she whispered to the boy and girl
dolls. "I'll be right here."

She put the father doll on the windowsill. "This is your new place," she said. "And you better have the kids come over to visit a lot—I'm telling you."

Then Casey climbed in bed with Elmer Elephant. After her mother had said good night to them, Casey whispered to Elmer, "Daddy says it's going to get better. Mommy says they still love us. So don't be scared, Elmer."

She snuggled closer to him and whispered "And I'll never leave you, Elmer. Never—ever."